D1558623

The Story of

The Grateful Crane

A Japanese Folktale Retold by JENNIFER BARTOLI

Illustrated Under the Direction of KOZO SHIMIZU

Albert Whitman Edition, 1977

Illustrations © 1972 Gakken Co., Ltd.

Printed in Japan

Albert Whitman & Company, Chicago

Once, when snow covered his valley,
an old man walked against the wind.
A farmer, he was on his way home
to his wife.

Climbing a small hill, he saw the red
crest of a crane in the snow. Its great wings
beat helplessly. The bird was trapped.

ROXHILL

Quickly the old man loosened the bird's leg, and quickly the bird flew away, free.

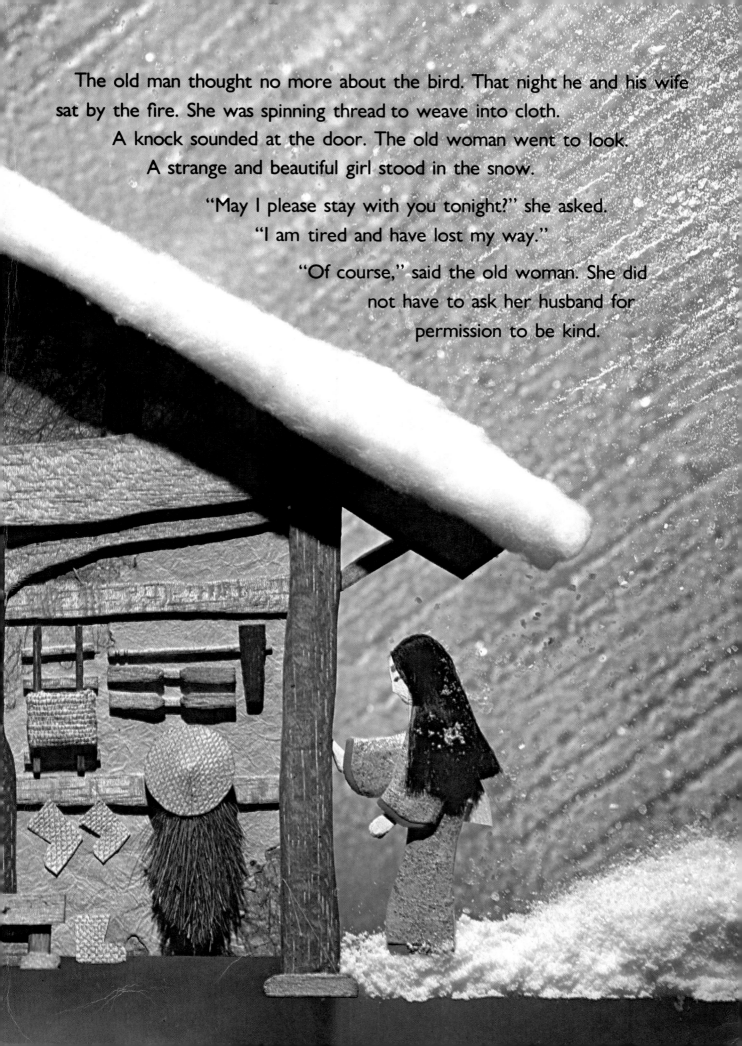

The old man thought no more about the bird. That night he and his wife
sat by the fire. She was spinning thread to weave into cloth.
A knock sounded at the door. The old woman went to look.
A strange and beautiful girl stood in the snow.

"May I please stay with you tonight?" she asked.
"I am tired and have lost my way."

"Of course," said the old woman. She did
not have to ask her husband for
permission to be kind.

In the morning, the snow was too deep for the girl to go on her way. She helped with the housework, and the old woman wove at her loom.

At supper, the girl spoke softly. "I have no father or mother. Let me live with you, and I will gladly be your daughter."

"How happy you make us!" said the old man. "We have no child of our own. Since you are tall and graceful like a crane, we will call you O-Tsuru."

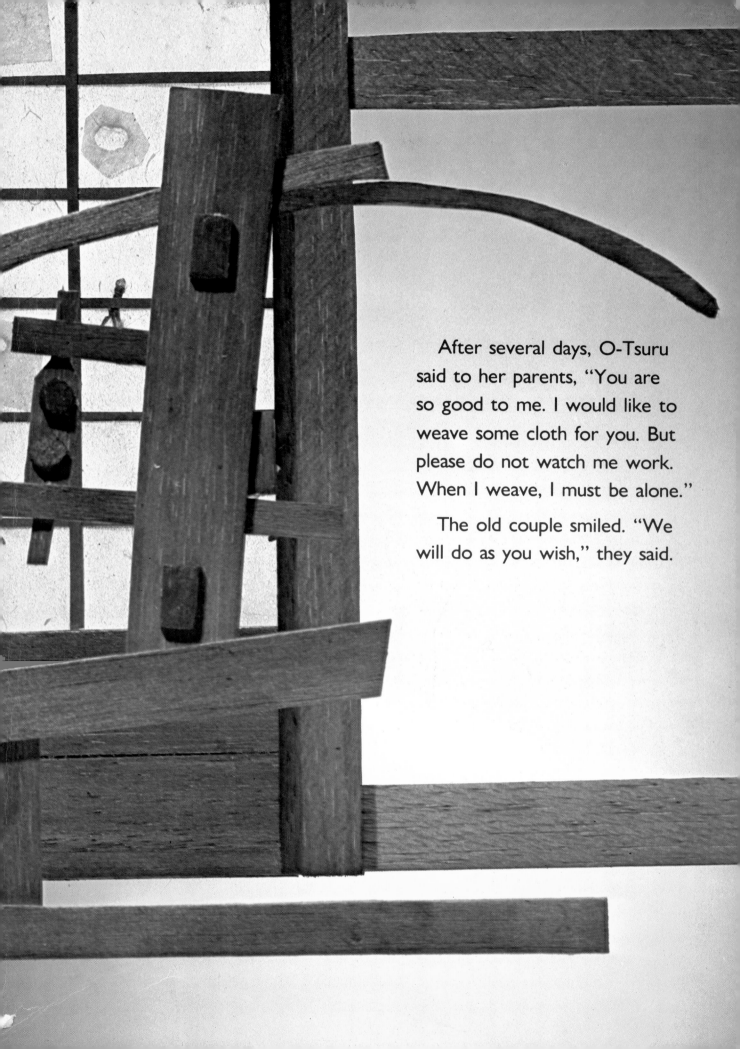

After several days, O-Tsuru
said to her parents, "You are
so good to me. I would like to
weave some cloth for you. But
please do not watch me work.
When I weave, I must be alone."

The old couple smiled. "We
will do as you wish," they said.

Without eating or sleeping, O-Tsuru worked through the day and into the night. The next morning, her parents still heard the old loom clicking and clacking.

"Never has our loom made this music," said the wife.

"No," said her husband. "But when will O-Tsuru rest? She must be tired."

For three days O-Tsuru worked on, and her parents listened and wondered. On the evening of the third day, their daughter came to them. A rainbow of colors filled the room.

"My father and mother," she said, "here is the cloth I promised you."

"Oh, how beautiful, O-Tsuru!" they exclaimed.

The girl bowed her head. "Thank you," she said.
"Sell this cloth and it will bring you gold."

A merchant from town came to look at the cloth. "I am sorry," he said. "I must go back. I need more gold to pay you for this fine silk."

He soon returned, with more gold than the old couple had ever seen.

O-Tsuru watched from the next room. She heard her parents ask, "How can we thank our daughter for all this gold?"

In the days that passed, the old couple did all they could to thank O-Tsuru.

Often the village children came to play with her. They loved O-Tsuru because she was patient and kind.

"It is good to see O-Tsuru play," the farmer told his wife. And she agreed.

One day O-Tsuru went again to the weaving room.
The old woman had promised not to watch, but she
was curious. While her husband looked on, she slid
open the doors.

A beautiful white crane worked alone at the loom.
Plucking its own feathers, the bird wove them into
silken cloth.

Then suddenly the crane was gone, and O-Tsuru stood before the old couple.

"I am not a girl, as you have believed," she said. She looked at the old man and went on, "I am the crane you once set free. You have loved me, and I am grateful. But now that you have seen me as I truly am, I must go."

"O-Tsuru," cried the old man and his wife.

But it was too late. Before their eyes,
O-Tsuru changed into a tall white crane.

"O-Tsuru, O-Tsuru!" they called.

Neither the old couple nor the children could bring her back. They stood silently in the snow and watched the white bird fly into the winter sunset.

With one farewell cry, O-Tsuru was gone.

A NOTE ABOUT THIS STORY

The tale of the grateful crane is familiar and well-loved in Japan but has appeared rarely in English translation. It illustrates a theme often repeated in Japanese folklore: how unwitting kindness to one of nature's creatures brings a reward, usually much needed. There is, for example, the story known by many names of the lowly cook on the fisherman's boat. He nightly tosses the day's leftovers into the sea and speaks kindly to the fish below. His generosity is repaid in gold.

Another familiar theme in folklore is found in the climax of the tale about the crane. Life's mysteries must not be examined too closely. This motif is present in Western as well as Eastern folk literature. The story of "The Elves and the Shoemaker" immediately comes to mind, as does the common superstition that one should not question good fortune lest it disappear. The fact that in the Japanese tale it is the old woman who gives in to her curiosity is also a frequent story element, recalling Pandora opening the box and suffering dire consequences.

The female figure that becomes a bird is present in art and literature. The bird is often associated with love, peace, and nurturing, traits attributed to women.

The illustrations, so meticulously reproduced from full-color photographs, are typical of a popular Japanese art form which uses low-relief sculpture. Paper, wood, and fabrics give this art a rich surface texture, and the models are arranged to make dramatic use of shadow.

Library of Congress Cataloging in Publication Data
Bartoli, Jennifer.
   The story of the grateful crane.

   SUMMARY: Retells the story of a crane who, when rescued from a trap by an old childless couple, repays their kindness in a magical way.
   [1. Folklore—Japan] I. Shimizu, Kōzō, 1925- II. Title.
PZ8.1.B313St   813'.5'4 [398.2]   77-3969
ISBN 0-8075-7630-1